Bekalu Wigglesworth was adopted from Ethiopia and joined his forever family on Christmas day, 2016. It took 19 government agencies, 10 trips, and 4 years to get him

This book is dedicated to Bekalu's
birth mother, who gave him life,
and the KVI nannies, who cared
for him his first 4 years of life

by **Laura Wigglesworth**

Illustrations by **Yuliya Somina**

Bekalu

From Ethiopia with love

4

Ethiopia, a land so far away
Was once my home, but not today.

Now I live with Molly and Claire
My sisters swing me in the air.

7

They teach me how to dance and sing
And from the diving board, to spring.

Before my family nannies I had
Who cared for me like a mom and dad.

They taught me how to crawl and walk
And later how to play and talk.

I miss the orphanage girls and boys
Together we made our own toys

15

We made things out of rocks and sticks
With string and plastic we did tricks.

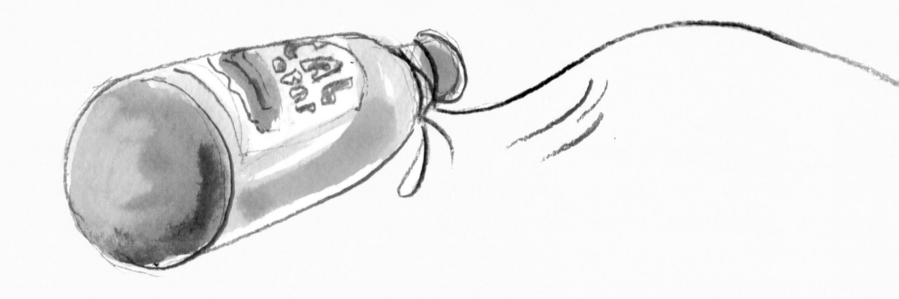

I'd swing a bottle 'round and round
Like a whip above the ground.

Sometimes I call my friends by phone
I wish they could come to my home.

21

I go to church on Sundays and pray
That all of my friends get a family some day.

ISBN -978-0-692-98820-6

CPSIA information can be obtained
at www.ICGtesting.com
Printed in the USA
BVXC01n0428121217
502585BV00028B/240